# Cold Keep

## by

## James Lovegrove

D1166932

First published in 2006 in Great Britain by
Barrington Stoke Ltd
www.barringtonstoke.co.uk

Copyright © 2006 James Lovegrove

The moral right of the author has been asserted in
accordance with the Copyright, Designs and
Patents Act 1988

ISBN 1-842993-63-1

Printed in Great Britain by Bell & Bain Ltd

# A Note from the Author

*Cold Keep* is set in the future, hundreds of years from now. The Earth is in the grip of a new Ice Age. Most of the planet is frozen over, though not all of it. A lot of modern technology doesn't work any more. It's a harsh world to live in. Yet people survive, even among the endless ice and snow.

The story is about Yana. She lives in a fortress city called Cold Keep. Cold Keep is in a remote place, hundreds of miles away from anywhere. All around, there is constant winter.

The walls of Cold Keep are made of rock and stone. They're very thick and tall. And they need to be thick and tall. Because there's danger just outside the walls. Out there are man-eating monsters known as the Shadow Trolls …

To Anna Gibbons

# Contents

# Chapter 1
# The Test

Yana stood on the tall outer wall of Cold Keep and watched the sun go down. The sun's rays turned the white landscape red. Snow and ice blazed, as if on fire.

Was this the last sunset Yana would ever see?

She gripped her axe tight. The blade and shaft of the axe were made from clear ice and were as strong as iron. The blade had been sharpened for her that afternoon. One of

Cold Keep's ice-smiths had poured water on it. As the water froze, the ice-smith had rubbed at the axe blade with a flat stone until its edge was razor sharp. The axe could cut through anything now. And it would not shatter.

When she held the axe Yana felt strong. Its strength gave her strength. It made her less afraid. For now.

But in less than half an hour's time Yana would be out on the snow, hunting, alone ...

Tonight was the night of Yana's Test. Tonight was the night when she proved she was a warrior, or died trying.

She looked round. Her teacher, Old Master Pav, was standing beside her. Yana had not heard him come up behind her. He could walk without making a sound. She was used to that, but even so she had a shock as she turned and suddenly saw him there.

"Are you nervous, Yana?" asked Old Master Pav.

"Of course not," Yana replied.

"I don't believe you." His eyes twinkled like the frost flakes that covered his beard and bushy eyebrows. "It's OK to be nervous before your Test. In fact, it's OK to be really scared."

"Were you scared when you did your Test, sir?"

Old Master Pav shook his head. "No," he said.

Somehow Yana wasn't surprised. She didn't think her teacher was scared of anything.

"No, I wasn't scared," he said. "I was petrified. It all happened a long time ago, and yet I can remember it as if it was yesterday. I stood up here on the high wall of Cold Keep, just where you're standing now. I was trembling so hard I thought I was going to crumble to bits. I watched the sun slip down behind those mountains there and I thought to myself, *Am I ever going to see it rise again?* But I did. I didn't die that night. I passed my Test. And you are going to pass yours, Yana. I'm sure of it.

"You've been in training for this night for nearly ten years," Old Master Pav went on. "Now you can show that all the training was worthwhile. You want to join the Grey Wolves, don't you? You want to become a defender of Cold Keep?"

"It's what I've wanted all my life," said Yana.

"Then you shall not fail."

"And if I do fail, I'll be dead, so it won't matter."

Old Master Pav nodded slowly. "That's true, I suppose. But listen to me, girl. I've never said this to you before, but I'll tell you now. You're a born warrior. I saw that the first day you came to me for training. Can you remember that day?"

"I was a little child," Yana said softly, "but I remember, of course."

"The first thing I did was hold out an axe to you, just like the one you have now. I wanted to see if you would take it from me with your bare hands. If you had, the ice would have stuck to your hands and would have ripped the skin off them. And what happened?"

"I put my gloves on."

"Exactly. Even though we were indoors, and warm, you knew the freezing ice would hurt your bare hands. I saw you were smarter than most people and that you would learn well. All my other pupils put their hands out for the axe without thinking. I had to pull the axe away from them quickly or else they'd have been badly hurt. You were different and I've always been sure that you would become a Grey Wolf. With every lesson, you've improved. You've worked hard to master all the combat skills. You've practised and practised to get things right. I've been hard on you. I've made you cry sometimes."

Yana turned her face away from Master Pav. She felt ashamed when she thought about how often she had broken down in tears during her training lessons. Sometimes she would get a move wrong. She would swing her axe up instead of down, or punch with her left hand instead of her right. Old Master Pav would tell her off. Yana would start to cry because she just *couldn't* get it right.

"You wanted to be the best," her teacher said, softly. "And I wanted you to be the best. Tonight, we'll see if you *are* the best."

He put his hand deep into his fur jacket.

"Here, I have a gift. Something to bring you luck."

He pulled an orange out of his pocket.

Yana looked at the fruit for a long time with greedy eyes. She had only seen an orange once before.

"For you," he said and gave it to her.

Yana put down her axe and took the orange. She held it up to her face and breathed in. The orange smelled tangy and sharp. It was a smell from the Warm Lands to the south, a smell from somewhere else, far away. The orange would taste delicious, Yana was sure. It would taste of sunshine and sweetness and hope.

"I can't accept this gift," she said at last. "It's too expensive."

She tried to give the orange back, but Old Master Pav shook his head.

"The orange can be your reason to survive," he said. "It will be your reward tomorrow morning, when you get back to Cold Keep alive."

"All right." Yana tucked the orange away inside her own fur jacket. "Did you buy it from the merchants who came last week?"

"I did."

"The same merchants who were attacked by the Trolls?"

"Yes."

Yana gave a grim smile. "Then I'll have to make sure the orange is safe this time too. That'll be my job tonight. I'll make sure the Shadow Trolls don't steal it *this* time."

Her teacher looked hard at Yana.

"The Shadow Trolls are not a joke, Yana. You know this. Be careful when you speak about them."

Yana looked down, embarrassed. "I'm sorry, sir."

"The Trolls are the enemy. They will always be the enemy. You must understand that."

"Yes, sir."

Old Master Pav watched his pupil for a moment. He was about to say something more, but just then the long, loud hoot of a horn sounded out across the Keep.

"Time to go," Master Pav said.

The sun had almost vanished. The sky was as red as blood. So was the snow.

Yana picked up her axe again and headed down to the gate.

# Chapter 2
# Outside

The massive gate was the only way into and out of Cold Keep. It was 20 metres high and weighed many tonnes. It took about 15 men to open and close it. They had to turn a gigantic wheel, which pulled a huge chain. The chain turned enormous cogs which slid the gate open. This gate was opened just twice a day, once in the morning and once in the evening.

Yana got to the gate just as it began to open. The ground rumbled. Splinters of ice showered down from the arch above the gate.

Before the gate was fully open, a line of workers from the quarry started tramping through. They had spent all day working to break up and collect rocks and stones. Their faces were worn and dusty. They looked glad that their shift was over and they were coming home. They sang a song as they entered Cold Keep. The chorus of the song went:

We've dug all day

We've worked like dogs

And now it's time to sleep

We'll have a drink

And go to bed

Snug inside Cold Keep

With the workers came some Grey Wolves. As they walked along, they held their axes at the ready. They had guarded the workers all day at the quarry and now were making sure they got back to Cold Keep safe and sound.

A few of the Grey Wolves spotted Yana and waved at her.

"Good luck," said one, with a wink.

"Bring back a Troll's head," said another.

When everyone had gone past, Yana stepped forwards. The gateway was huge and she felt very small. She turned round. The workers and Grey Wolves were going off in different directions, down the narrow, twisty streets of the fortress city. Soon they had vanished.

Old Master Pav had said he would not walk with Yana to the gate. He didn't like saying goodbye to his pupils when they went to face their Tests.

Yana's parents had died when she was very small. There was only her older brother, Jorn. But he wasn't at Cold Keep any more. He had left three years ago. He went away to start a new life in the Warm Lands, and Yana had not heard from him since.

So there was nobody to say goodbye to her.

The horn hooted again. That meant that the gate was about to close.

Yana kept on walking towards it. As the gate began to slide shut, she wanted more than anything to run back. She made herself keep on walking. At last, the gate slammed shut with a huge ringing *clang*. Yana was shut out of Cold Keep now. She promised herself that she would be alive to walk back through the gate when it opened again tomorrow morning.

She didn't look back at Cold Keep until she had walked almost a kilometre across the snow. When she did, she saw the giant walls and turrets. They towered against the stars and shone blackly like a dark, glittering jewel. Here and there, the snow lay in drifts against the outer walls, frozen hard. The frozen drifts looked like huge white claws that had risen from the earth around Cold Keep to hold it in place. It looked as if the ice was gripping the fortress city and would never let go.

Yana went on walking. The next time she looked back, Cold Keep seemed so small and far away.

Wind whistled around her and swirled the snowflakes at her feet. The moon had risen and was bright and full. Yana could see almost as well as if it was daytime. Everything glowed in the moonlight.

She trudged onward.

Yana had taken the road that led south, away from Cold Keep. It was the only road that went anywhere but it was buried by snow almost all year. You could see where the road went because there were two-metre-high pillars set along its sides.

As well as the pillars, Yana could see where the road was because of the tracks which the merchants' sledges had made the week before. The sledges had cut deep into the snow because they were loaded with heavy slabs of stone they'd taken back South. The merchants brought food to Cold Keep from the South – like oranges and tea – and took stone slabs back in exchange. But by the time the next lot of merchants came, a month from now, the tracks would be covered up by the snow again.

Would the snow cover Yana's body too, if she died tonight?

She told herself not to think that way. She was freezing cold already and shivering. There was no need to make it worse by thinking about what would happen to her dead body.

*You're going to pass the Test*, Old Master Pav had told her. *I'm sure of it.*

Yana prayed he was right.

# Chapter 3
# Screaming Crag

Soon, sooner than she would have liked, Yana reached Screaming Crag.

It was here that just last week the Shadow Trolls had attacked the merchants. The Trolls had hidden below the crag, among the rocks.  Then they had jumped up from their hiding place and come running out with howls and grunts.  Their blue-black cloaks flapped behind them as they ran to attack the merchants.  There were at least ten of them, the merchants said.  It had been terrifying.

A band of Grey Wolves was with the merchants to guard them.  They clashed with the Shadow Trolls and drove them away.  The Grey Wolves ran after them, but the Trolls had fled behind Screaming Crag and vanished.  The Grey Wolves knew that the Trolls had a hide-out somewhere nearby.  For many years they had tried to find it, with no luck.  Was it in a cave with a secret entrance, or in a hole hidden in the ground?  Nobody could say.

Yana looked up at Screaming Crag.  It was a ridge of solid rock which jutted straight up from the snow like a cliff.  The sides were steep and slippery and the top was zig-zags of rock.  Sometimes when you looked up at it, it was as if the crag was made of stone people.  The rocks looked like a crowd of giants, with their legs and arms all twisted, their heads back and their mouths open and screaming.  A crowd of giants in agony.  Of course, the crag was just rocks, but once you'd seen them as giants, it was difficult *not* to see them like that for ever.

Yana looked down now to the bottom of the crag. Were there Shadow Trolls crouched there right now, silently watching her?

She took her axe and held it ready. She went on walking along the road, but she kept watching Screaming Crag. A few times she thought she saw something move at the bottom of the crag. Maybe she just imagined it. Maybe not. Even with the bright moonlight she couldn't be sure.

At Cold Keep, people didn't talk much about the Shadow Trolls, and when they did they talked in whispers. No-one wanted to talk about the Trolls. Somehow, talking about them seemed to bring them out into the open. Often, if someone talked about the Trolls too loudly, one would be spotted the next day. A

Grey Wolf guard would see one on the horizon, or a Grey Wolf hunting party would come home and say they'd had a run-in with a group of Trolls out in the snow.

So you said nothing about the Shadow Trolls. That way, maybe the Trolls would stay away from Cold Keep.

All the same, Yana had heard all about them. She knew what people said they were, or *thought* they were.

Some people said the Trolls used to be humans. Long ago, before the Eternal Winter began, the Trolls had been a group of weather scientists. They had been working here in the far north and had got stranded, cut off by snow. They had survived by becoming cannibals. They had many children who were born wilder and more dangerous every year. Now, hundreds of years on, the Trolls were hardly human any more.

Other people said they were monsters, pure and simple. They lived underground and had always liked to eat human flesh. If they couldn't find seals or arctic foxes to eat, then they were happy to eat humans. There were many old stories about them, calling them different names – trolls or even demons.

Whether the Shadow Trolls were demons or humans gone wild, one thing was sure. The people of Cold Keep were scared of them. Children were told never to go outside Cold Keep alone and never to leave the fortress city after dark. That was when the Trolls liked to hunt. Everyone knew about children who'd been snatched away by Trolls. Adults were too. You were safe as long as you stayed near Cold Keep. The Trolls were scared of the bows and arrows of the Grey Wolf guards. But if you strayed too far, you might well be taken prisoner and end up as supper for the Shadow Trolls …

Jorn, Yana's brother, had said he couldn't stand the way everyone was so scared of the Trolls. It was as if the people who lived in Cold Keep were prisoners. That was one of the things that made him go South. Why should he have to stay trapped in the fortress city, afraid to set foot outside? It wasn't fair.

He thought, too, that he would have a better life down in the Warm Lands. He would be free. He wouldn't have to work in the quarry. He would lie in warm sunshine and swim in a warm sea. He would never again have to put up with the long, long nights of the winter months.

He had tried to make Yana come with him. His plan was to stow away, to hide on the back of a merchant's sledge.

"We'll both go," he had said. "We can start a new life in the Warm Lands. We'll pick oranges and bananas for a living, or grow sugar cane, or look after chickens, something like that. It'll be a second chance for us. It'll be great!"

But Yana had said no. She couldn't leave. What about her training? What about her dream of becoming a Grey Wolf?

"Forget them. Forget your training," her brother had said with a laugh. "It's a waste of time. Do you want to spend the rest of your life stuck here? Do you want to live in a tiny flat with no windows, with just a feeble solar panel to heat your food and your water? Do you want to be miserable and cold and wear ten layers of clothing every day till you die? Is that all you want?"

"Yes," Yana had replied firmly, "it is."

"You're so stubborn, Yana." But Jorn had said that as a compliment, as well as an insult.

When the next lot of merchants came, Jorn had done what he'd said he would. When the merchants left Cold Keep, he was hidden in their sledges. Now he was gone. Yana didn't know what sort of new life Jorn had made for himself in the Warm Lands. She'd heard that it was difficult to find a job and make money down there. Everyone wanted to be in the Warm Lands, but there wasn't a lot of space. There weren't enough houses or jobs for all the people who lived there. The Warm Lands were crowded and cruel. You could get beaten up just for looking at someone in the wrong way. You could get killed if you had a job or some food which someone else felt belonged to *them*.

Yana thought that, after all, she was better off at Cold Keep. It might not be the safest place in the world, but then the Warm Lands weren't as great as Jorn seemed to think.

She nearly laughed at that thought. Safe? Right now, as she tracked Shadow Trolls, she was anything *but* safe.

Suddenly Yana heard a thumping sound behind her.

She wheeled round.  She was sure she'd see a Shadow Troll rushing towards her. Maybe more than one of them.  Maybe a few.

In fact, it wasn't a Troll.

In many ways, it was worse.

# Chapter 4

# Polar Bear

The polar bear moved fast, lolloping across the snow.

Polar bears were big, clumsy animals. They looked as if they were so heavy, they could hardly run. But they could. When they got up speed, they could go as fast as a human could sprint.

This one was hungry. It was looking for prey and it had found Yana. It was coming to get her. It looked like a shaggy mountain of white fur. Its eyes glittered like coals.

Yana knew she had to run but she couldn't get her body to move. Seeing the polar bear seemed to have sent her into shock. All she could do was stare at the bear as it raced in for the kill.

Finally, something clicked in her head. Yana was able to move. She dived sideways just as the polar bear got to her. The bear was going too quickly to change direction in time. It shot past her. Yana rolled over on the ground.

She was back on her feet at once and running. Running as hard as she could, still holding onto her axe.

The polar bear skidded round and chased after her. Its enormous paws thudded on the snow.

Yana put her head down and kept going. She could hear the bear. She was running flat out but the bear was just behind her. Her feet sank into the snow, sometimes up to the ankle. She nearly fell. If she fell, the polar bear would pounce and that would be that.

She was making for Screaming Crag. That was the only place she could think of where she stood a chance of escaping the bear. At that moment she didn't care that the crag was where the Shadow Trolls liked to hide. The only thing that mattered was not getting ripped to bits by the bear's claws and fangs.

Screaming Crag loomed in front of her. She got to the rocks below it and started to scramble up them. She held her axe in one hand and used her other hand to help her climb. The rocks were very slippery. It was hard to keep going, but Yana didn't stop. She slithered, cracked her knees, bruised her shins, banged her elbows, but she kept on climbing.

The bear couldn't follow. It tried to, but it couldn't get over the rocks. It snarled as it looked for a way to catch up with Yana. It lumbered up onto the rocks but fell backwards again and again. Yana had got away. The bear was angry. It shook its head.

When Yana could not climb any further, she sat and looked back down at the bear. She was at the top of the rocks now. This was where the steep cliff-face of the crag began. The bear was 50 metres below. It paced to and fro, still snarling at Yana. In the end, it settled down on the snow to wait.

Yana knew she was in trouble. She was safe from the bear for now, but the bear had decided to sit and wait. It knew she was stuck. She couldn't go any higher. She couldn't climb the cliff-face of the crag.

The polar bear would wait. Sooner or later, Yana would have to come back down the crag.

Then the bear could attack again.

# Chapter 5
# A Choice of Deaths

Time passed. Yana didn't know how long. Perhaps an hour.

The cold began to seep through her clothes to her skin. She moved about to try and stay warm. She stretched her legs and waved her arms around. She knew she had to keep her heart pumping. She had to make sure her blood kept warm inside her. Otherwise she would get frostbite.

Walking would have been the best thing, better than what she was doing now. But there was nowhere to go, no room for walking. While she was up here on the rocks, all she could do was stretch her arms and legs out. She couldn't even jump up and down on the spot. There were too many rocks.

She thought she could last a few hours like this. But unless the bear got bored and went away, a few hours was all she had. She knew that then the sub-zero temperatures would start to get to her. She would freeze to death. Her thoughts would become sluggish. Her body would start to go numb. She would fall into a sort of sleep and drift away.

Dying of cold was supposed to be a peaceful death. But that wasn't much comfort to Yana.

There was something else she could do, but she would die even sooner.

31

She remembered some advice which Old Master Pav had given her about polar bears.

"It's very simple," he had said. "Never get into a fight with one. You will not win. You will always, always come off worst. A single person against a polar bear? My money is on the bear."

But here and now, she had no choice.

Either she died a slow death up here on the rocks, or she went down to fight the bear and died quickly. Maybe, just maybe, she might be able to kill the bear. But there wasn't much of a chance of that.

Yana thought about what she should do.

In the end, it was no choice at all.

She stood up and began to make her way down.

When the polar bear saw this, it got up too. It stamped on the snow with one of its

---

front paws, showing that it was ready to meet her.

Then, all at once, it lifted its nose and sniffed. It had smelled something or heard something. It had noticed something else.

The next instant, the bear swung round and loped off. Yana watched it go, puzzled. The bear looked alarmed. It jogged towards the horizon. It became a white dot and then Yana couldn't see it any more.

What had startled the bear? What could make an animal as big and dangerous as a polar bear turn round and flee?

Yana didn't want to know. And yet she had a horrible feeling she *did* know.

To her right, she saw some dark figures coming across the snow. There were about five or six of them. Their steps were slow and steady and strong.

The bear had known they were coming and knew it couldn't win against so many. It was outnumbered.

So was Yana.

But she had nowhere to go.

And the dark figures were Shadow Trolls.

# Chapter 6

# Shadow Trolls

Yana had never seen Shadow Trolls before in her life. But she still knew that was what they were. The figures were hunched but man-like. They had dark, ragged cloaks with hoods. They were out at night on the snow. What else could they be?

The Shadow Trolls hadn't seen her yet, as far as she could tell. She ducked behind a rock and peeked at them over the top.

She was very scared. Her mouth had gone dry and her heart was thumping. But she felt something else too. Excitement. The Shadow Trolls were what would test her. All she had to do was kill them. Then she would become a Grey Wolf. She could wear the badge of a Grey Wolf, and the seal-skin sash. She would carry a bow and arrow as well as an ice axe. She would be able to live with the Grey Wolves and join in their night parties when they came back from a day out on the ice. The people who lived in Cold Keep would treat her with respect. They would call her "*Brave Guard*" and not just "*Yana*" or "*You, Girl*".

All at once, killing a few Shadow Trolls seemed worth it, a small thing to do. And a *good* thing to do.

The Trolls were moving away now. Yana slid out from behind the rock and picked her way down to the snow.

By the time she got there, she couldn't see the Trolls any more. They had gone round the side of Screaming Crag. That didn't matter. Yana could follow their tracks in the snow.

She set off after the Trolls at a steady pace.

# Chapter 7
# Ambush

As she followed the Shadow Trolls' trail, Yana heard Old Master Pav's advice in her head.

"They're hard to track," he had said. "They can and will trick you. They can flow like darkness. They can float like the wind. They will do what you least expect."

Yana remembered this but she wasn't sure if it was true. The Shadow Trolls weren't being very tricky right now. They were leaving such clear tracks that even a child could follow them. The marks which their feet made in the snow stood out as if they were lit up. Yana had no problem following the trail, even if the Trolls were too far ahead for her to see.

It was like that for two or three kilometres. Yana followed the Trolls across snowfield after snowfield. The stars glittered like diamonds overhead. The moon shone down like a fat, perfect pearl. Yana hoped to catch the Trolls when they stopped for a rest. She would sneak up on them, just as Old Master Pav had taught her. She would surprise them. Then she would be able to kill at least three of them before the others even saw her.

A fire of excitement burned in her belly.

Then, just like that, the tracks ended.

The Shadow Trolls had walked onto a glacier, a frozen lake. There was nothing but

solid ice underfoot.  No snow, so no
footprints.

The fire inside her died and turned to
ashes.  Everything had been going so well
until now.

But still Yana kept walking.  She moved
over the ice with care.  She put her feet down
slowly, toe then heel, so as not to slip over.

She arrived at a spot where some black
rocks jutted up through the ice of the glacier.
The rocks were all the same size.  Each was a
round lump not much bigger than a sack of
coal.  Yana waited for a moment to think.
Had she lost track of the Trolls?  Had they got
away?  Had they known all along that she was
behind them?  Perhaps they *were* as tricky as
Old Master Pav had said, after all.

Yana ground her teeth in anger.  She
lowered her axe, resting its head on one of
the rocks.

One of the rocks shuddered.

All at once it came alive. It turned into a human being, or into something *like* a human being.

All the other rocks did the same.

The Shadow Trolls leapt to their feet around Yana. They had been crouching down and had used their cloaks to cover themselves and make themselves look like rocks.

Yana looked left, looked right.

In a circle around her, monster faces glared back.

# Chapter 8
# Claws

Yana couldn't see the Trolls properly. The hoods of their cloaks fell over their faces and hid them. What Yana could see was ugly and distorted. They had noses and cheeks and mouths. But the noses were lumpy, the cheeks weren't level with each other, and the mouths were narrow, twisted slits.

Worst of all were the eyes.

The Trolls' eyes were black and hollow, like the empty eye sockets of a skull. They stared at Yana. There was no life in them, no pity, nothing.

Then one of the Trolls grunted. The others answered, also grunting.

All at once Yana came to her senses. She remembered who she was and why she was here.

Old Master Pav's training kicked in. Yana went calm inside. She understood now the point of every lesson she had had with her teacher. Everything led up to this moment.

She let out a breath and swung her axe at the nearest Troll.

The blow missed. The Troll dived out of the way. Yana swung again. The axe whirled through the air. She was aiming for the same Troll, but it was fast on its feet. She missed again. She went for it a third time, using a downward strike. The Troll leapt back and her axe blade hit the icy ground. Chips of ice

shot in all directions. Yana's arms shook
with the force of the blow.

She lifted the axe for a fresh attack, but
then one of the other Trolls tackled her from
the side. It was hard to keep her footing on
the glacier. Yana crashed to the ground on
her back, with the Troll on top of her.

That was when she saw its claws.

Shadow Trolls didn't carry any weapons.
They didn't need to. What they had were the
claws. They were hook-shaped and stood out
on the end of their fingers. Each claw was at
least five centimetres long. With these they
could dig into the flesh of their victims. It
was said that the talons could even cut
through bone.

The Troll on top of Yana lifted its arm.
She looked up at five points, wicked and sharp
in the air above her. The claws were above
her face, ready to come down and slash it to
ribbons.

She was still holding her axe. There wasn't time to use it properly. Instead, Yana swung it sideways and hit the Troll's head with the flat of the blade.

The Troll let out a yelp and rolled off her.

Yana sprang back to her feet.

Two of the other Trolls rushed at her with their claws out. One of them grabbed her axe by its handle, while the other drove its shoulder into her stomach. Yana fell to the ground again, gasping for air.

The Troll sat on top of her. This time Yana did not have her axe. The other Troll had snatched it off her. This time she had only her arms and legs and her strength.

Yana punched the Troll before it could sink its claws into her. She hit its chest and belly, as hard as she could. She kept punching the Troll so that it didn't have the chance to fight back. Then she shoved her knees up between her and the Troll. She pushed and flipped the Troll over her head. The Troll crash-landed on the ice. It let out a groan that sounded almost human.

Yana stood up. The other Trolls closed in on her, with evil grunts. She looked around for her axe. It was lying on the ice behind the Trolls and she couldn't get to it.

She had no weapon. There were four Trolls and only one of her.

Yana did the only thing she could.

She turned and ran.

# Chapter 9
# The Ice Bridge

Yana wasn't running away from the Shadow Trolls. She wasn't a coward. She wanted them to follow her, and she needed her axe back.

Her plan was to go round in a big circle on the ice. The Trolls would leave her axe, then she could return to it and get to it before they did. She didn't have a hope against them without her axe.

She was running so hard, she nearly fell into a crevasse. She skidded to a halt just in time.

The crevasse was a deep split in the ice. It was ten metres wide and went right down a hundred metres or more. Yana couldn't see the bottom. It was lost in darkness.

The crevasse stretched in a line in front of her, in both directions as far as she could see. There was no way she could jump across it. How was she going to get to the other side? The Trolls were behind her.

Then Yana spotted something not far away. It was a bridge made of ice which linked the two sides of the crevasse. She ran to it. The bridge looked thin, and the thinnest part was in the middle. It could easily snap. Could she use to it cross the crevasse?

There was no other way. The Trolls had almost caught up with her. She could see them out of the corner of her eye. They were charging towards her. She could hear their horrible grunts.

She stepped onto the ice bridge. She moved as quickly as she could. The bridge creaked and cracked as she darted across. Icicles which hung underneath it broke off and fell into the crevasse. Yana held her breath. She made herself feel as if she was as light as a bird.

She jumped the last few metres and threw herself onto the ice at the far end of the bridge. She lay flat on her front and she looked back behind her shoulder. One of the Trolls was already putting a foot onto the bridge. It was doing this in a very careful way. Yana had gone over the bridge as fast as she could but the Troll came across more slowly.

Yana stood up. She had had an idea.

She stamped on her end of the bridge. The ice bridge was already fragile. Yana had made it more fragile when she ran across it. A few hard kicks would make the bridge shatter.

It did. It broke away in chunks, starting at the place where Yana was stamping. The ice bridge fell bit by bit, one piece after another and crashed into the crevasse with a noise like rolling thunder.

The Troll was standing on the far end of the bridge. That was the last piece to go. The Troll would have crashed down into the crevasse as well, but two of the other Trolls caught it in time. They grabbed it by the arms and saved it from falling. They pulled it back up onto the rim of the crevasse.

Now the crevasse lay between Yana and the Shadow Trolls. But her axe was on the other side, behind them. Added to that, she was lost. She wasn't sure where she was any more.

How could she get back to Cold Keep?

# Chapter 10
# The Weather Station

Yana walked over and around the ice for a few hours. She felt confused and miserable. Nothing had gone the way it was meant to. She hadn't killed any Trolls, and she had lost her axe. She was sure she had failed her Test. To make things worse, a wind had got up. It blew snowflakes into her eyes, which stung. Yana pulled on the strings of her hood to make it tighter and kept on walking.

She came across the group of huts by accident. They were half buried in the snow. There were three or four of them and they had curved roofs and tiny round windows in the walls. She had never seen anything like them before and couldn't work out what they were. The huts were very small and fragile, nothing like Cold Keep.

Yana thought she could shelter in one for a while. She found a door at the end of one of the huts. It was odd because it looked as if someone else had been there too, that same night. There were footprints around the door and marks in the snow where someone had opened it.

Did somebody live here? Who?

Yana wasn't sure if she should go inside. But the wind was cutting into her like a knife. It would be nice to be indoors for a while. She could wait in the hut till sunrise. Maybe the footprints weren't new. Maybe no-one had been inside the hut for a long time.

She pulled the door open and entered.

She soon got used to the gloom inside. Moonlight came in through the tiny round windows. Everything had a faint, silvery glow. Yana saw tables, chairs and bunk beds. There were other things too – things with wires and switches, handles and rods. Everything was broken and dusty. Yana didn't know what these things were but she soon worked it out.

They must be all sorts of measuring tools to record the weather and temperature. There were scopes to look at the sky and apparatus to measure air pressure. There were jugs with weird markings on the side. There was even something which Yana thought must be a "computer". She had once heard about "computers". People had used them a lot, back in the past before the

Eternal Winter began. Computers had been like brains, doing very complicated thinking. The thing Yana thought was a computer was like a window inside a box, with a tray attached to it. The tray was covered with letters of the alphabet.

Yana knew what this place must be. The buildings were a weather station. There had been scientists here, long ago. They had been here to record facts about the weather.

*The scientists must be the very same ones who became Shadow Trolls.*

Yana recalled the footprints outside the door. They weren't old at all. She knew that now. They couldn't be old. If they were old, the snow would have covered them up ages ago.

This was it! This was where the Shadow Trolls lived! She had found out where they went to whenever they vanished.

Yana spun round. She must leave right away. The Trolls she had just fought with would be coming back this way, once they had gone round the crevasse. They would be here soon. They could even be outside the door right now ...

In her panic, Yana banged into something on the table. It was a cardboard box. It fell onto the floor and everything that was in it spilled out.

She looked down. There was a heap of dark cloth. And in the middle of the heap was a face.

It was a horrible face.

It was the face of a Shadow Troll.

It stared up at her with empty eyes and twisted mouth.

Yana took a step back in shock. She couldn't work out what the face was doing there on the floor. Something wasn't right about this. How come it was just the Troll's face there, nothing else?

She prodded the face with the tip of her boot. The face was hard and hollow. She nudged the cloth it was lying on, also with the tip of her boot.

A hand fell out.

She knew that hand. She knew the claws. Just a little while ago some claws just like those had hung above her face, ready to tear it to shreds.

In fact it wasn't a hand at all. It was a glove, with claws stuck on the fingers. All the things that lay on the floor in a heap were clothes – gloves and cloaks with hoods.

Yana knelt down and picked up the Troll's face. The eyes were two holes, covered in thin, dark cotton. She turned the face around and held it up in front of her own face. She could just see through the eye-holes.

The face was a mask.

Just as Yana was beginning to understand what all this meant, the door opened. Wind hissed into the building.

Then she heard a voice she knew very well.

"So there it is, Yana," said Old Master Pav. "You've found out the truth."

# Chapter 11
# The Truth

Old Master Pav took off the Troll mask he was wearing.  He pulled off the gloves with the claws on the fingers.  He threw back the hood of his Shadow Troll cloak.

Behind him the other Shadow Trolls did the same.  Yana was looking at six human beings, not six monsters.  She knew their real faces.  They were all Grey Wolves, like Old Master Pav.

"You ... you're the Shadow Trolls," she stammered. "You dress up to look like them."

"Indeed," said Old Master Pav.

"So there aren't any Trolls. Not really."

"There aren't. There's just us and these clothes we wear. There never have been any Trolls."

Yana had trouble asking her next question. "But why?"

"Why?" Her teacher thought for a moment. "Because there needs to be an enemy out there. Without one, people wouldn't want to stay at Cold Keep. If they did stay they would argue and fight among themselves. Life would be far more difficult. The Shadow Trolls make sure that everyone has something to be afraid of. If there's an enemy that everyone's scared of, we can all stay together and get on with things. It's that simple."

"So this is all just a big *game*? You pretend to be Shadow Trolls, and the other Grey Wolves pretend to fight you and guard everyone against you."

"It's not a game, Yana. It's been going on too long for that. It's how Cold Keep stays safe and calm. It's how Cold Keep exists. With no enemy outside to be scared of, many more people would leave, like your brother did. They'd go off a few at a time until there was no-one left. But as long as everyone thinks the Shadow Trolls are prowling around outside, people stay safe inside and only leave to go to the quarry. Cold Keep is important, you see."

"What, because we have all that stone and rock to trade with?"

"Yes, but also because we're proof. Proof that you don't *have* to live in the Warm Lands. Proof that people can live even up here in the snow and ice. We can survive anything."

Yana was having trouble hiding her dismay and her anger. Everything she believed in was shattered.

"I know this is all a bit of a shock," Old Master Pav said. "I also know that you're a smart enough girl to understand why we do what we do."

"What about my Test?" Yana said. "Was that fake too? Was all my training a waste of time?"

"Not at all. You passed your Test with flying colours. You fought us without any fear. You nearly killed one of us."

"My ears are still ringing," said one of the Grey Wolves. He must have been the Troll she had hit on the side of the head.

"And I'm damn lucky I didn't end up at the bottom of that crevasse," said one of the female Grey Wolves.

"You were fantastic, Yana. I'm proud of you," said Old Master Pav. "You were clever. You thought on your feet. You were dangerous even after I took your axe off you. And to finish everything off, you found this hut, where we keep our Shadow Troll outfits."

"That was just luck."

"Even so, I'd say you did well. If we were giving out marks, you'd get an A. But apart from all that, there's something very important you need to think about."

Yana frowned at him.

Old Master Pav looked very serious. "You have to decide what you're going to do now, Yana. You have to tell us if you're going to join us or not. That's very important."

"What happens if I *don't* join you?" Yana asked.

"What do you think?"

"You kill me."

"Oh no." Her teacher gave a small, sad smile. "We'd never do that. What we do is march you down to the South and leave you there. It's too far to return to Cold Keep on your own. You'd never make it."

"You banish me."

"That's it."

"I could always come back with the merchants," Yana said.

"Why do you think the Grey Wolves always guard the merchants?" asked Master Pav. "Can't you see? That's when we check who they've got with them. Once you've left Cold Keep, there's no coming back."

"So that's my choice," Yana said. "I can join in this ... this *trick* of yours. Or I can go South and never return."

"Yes, Yana. That's your choice. So, which is it to be?"

# Chapter 12
# The Orange

The sunrise was coming.  There was a purple glow in the east.  The stars were growing dim.  The moon had gone.

Yana sat outside the huts, alone, thinking.

She had been sitting there ever since Old Master Pav had arrived.  He was still indoors with the other Grey Wolves.  They had all changed out of their Shadow Troll costumes and were melting snow on a small stove to make tea.

Yana didn't know what to do. How could she decide? On the one hand, the Shadow Trolls were a great big lie. This meant everything she had believed in and longed for was a great big lie. What was the point of being a warrior when you had to play at being the enemy as well? Why become a Grey Wolf if Shadow Trolls didn't exist?

On the other hand, if she didn't become a Grey Wolf, Yana would have to leave Cold Keep. She would be thrown out of her home, unable to return.

The Test had been thrilling. Now it was over, Yana looked back and didn't remember the fear she'd felt. She remembered only the excitement of getting the better of the Trolls.

But she saw the purpose of the Test wasn't to prove her skill as a warrior. It was to make her want to belong with the Grey Wolves. It was to make her feel that she had earned the right to be a part of their nasty secret.

She felt angry, let down and alone.

She hugged herself to stay warm. As she did so, she felt a hard lump inside her jacket. Something small, hard and round was pressing against her ribs.

It was the orange which Old Master Pav had given her. She had forgotten all about it.

She took it out of her pocket. She held it in her hands. She was tired after everything that had happened that night. She was hungry, too. As she looked at the orange, her mouth began to water.

Yana thought of the Warm Lands where the orange came from and where Jorn was now. Was he waiting for her to go there to be with him? Was he still alive?

Suddenly the orange seemed to be a sign of a new life in the Warm Lands. It was the second chance that Jorn had talked about.

But the orange was also a gift from Old Master Pav. It was a kind gift and very expensive. Any sort of fruit was a rare luxury in Cold Keep. It must have cost Master Pav at least a week's wages, even though he was a Grey Wolf and well paid.

*If I eat the orange*, Yana thought, *I'll be accepting that my future lies here at Cold Keep, with the Grey Wolves. But if I don't eat it, then,* thought Yana, *my future lies in the Warm Lands where Jorn has gone.*

The sun came up onto the horizon. It nudged up slowly, a shimmering, golden circle. Brilliant light flooded the sky. The snow sparkled, so dazzling that it made Yana blink. A beautiful dawn.

Home, and a lie? Or South, to a place she knew nothing about?

If she stayed, Yana would be one of the rulers of Cold Keep.  She would be given all the best things that Cold Keep had to offer.  If she went South, she would be just another person in the struggle to survive.

Old Master Pav had played a cruel trick on her.  But he hadn't wanted her to be hurt.  He wanted her to have a good life.

With a deep sigh, Yana took off one of her gloves.  She dug her thumb nail into the orange and began to tear off the peel.

Barrington Stoke would like to thank all its readers for commenting on the manuscript before publication and in particular:

Jade Bason

Sarah-Frances Bateson

Craig Carroll

J Carss

Mrs Carter-Brown

Jade Cross

Danielle Deller

Jonathan Druce

Luke Gale

Tom Goodwin

Diane Hayes

Adrian Kelly

Melanie Maben

Mrs J. McCreave

Dhani Parry

Mrs Linda Paterson

Ben Pringle

Lizzy Putnam

Sophie Rogerson

Becky Talbot

Stacey Turner

Peter Walton

## Become a Consultant!

Would you like to give us feedback on our titles before they are published? Contact us at the email address below – we'd love to hear from you!

info@barringtonstoke.co.uk
www.barringtonstoke.co.uk

If you loved this book, why don't you read ...

# Ant God

## by James Lovegrove

ISBN 1-842993-29-1

Big ideas. Big and weird ideas. That's what Dan's best friend Jason does best. Like the one when he decided that cats ruled the world. Now he's made the Truth Glasses. He says they show him things ... things that shouldn't be seen.

You can order *Ant God* directly from our website at **www.barringtonstoke.co.uk**

If you loved this book, why
don't you read ...

# Wings

## by James Lovegrove

ISBN 1-842991-93-0

Az dreams of being like everyone else.
In the world of the Airborn that means
growing wings. It seems impossible, but
with an inventor for a father, who knows?

You can order *Wings* directly from our website at
www.barringtonstoke.co.uk

If you loved this book, why don't you read ...

# The House of Lazarus

## by James Lovegrove

ISBN 1-842991-25-6

Joey's mum didn't want to die. So she made Joey promise to rent her a place at the House of Lazarus, where they say they can keep people alive for ever. It costs a lot to keep her there and Joey finds it hard to pay the rent. Then he has a strange dream and begins to wonder if he has done the right thing. Can the House of Lazarus really give people the gift of eternal life?

You can order *The House of Lazarus* directly from our website at **www.barringtonstoke.co.uk**